Rage

by Paul Rowbotham

Publisher: Authentic Worth

ISBN 978-1-8381693-0-5

For more information about workshops, resources and author bookings relating to Rage visit

www.reading4life.co.uk

This book is dedicated to all the young people I have worked with over my 25 years of teaching - Keisha Stewart, the book's illustrator, being one of them. It has been a privilege to learn from so many of these young minds. Their zest for life never ceases to amaze me.

Resilience is a quality I see in so many of these young people as they strive through their challenges - whatever shape or form they take.

I hope that this book will inspire its readers to face their inner fears, unravel the complexities of their emotions and find their 'Aliya' – a friend who makes a difference.

One:

Time to Run

Rage has many colours. Most see red, but then there's yellow, purple and even green. The colours change too, like a sky at sunset – the artist paints it one way, then another, until the perfect atmosphere is captured. Rage is never perfect though and when one sees red, they actually see no colours at all. All the senses are nullified.

Claire had had enough. *What the Hell!* She was screaming - the voices echoing inside her head. She didn't want anyone to know. She had her dignity. *I'm not sharing these tears with anyone. They can stuff it.*

What happened next surprised Claire, her teacher and all her classmates. The computer screen landed with an almighty crash. She had lifted it above her head, with cables dangling like tentacles, paused, looked around and then brought it hurtling down. If it had been basketball, it would have been one mighty slam-dunk.

Time to run. Claire hopped over the screen and made a dash for the classroom door. Expecting someone to chase her and tackle her to the ground, she felt a surge of energy. Turning her head, though, she noticed no one had moved. Everyone was still sitting there, frozen by the shock of what had just happened. *I need somewhere safe.* Her brain did a quick scan of the school: *The ground floor would be safest. Better still, get out of the building.* She ran down the nearest stairs and then, realising no one was behind her, started to walk. She saw another teacher approaching and decided to walk on, feigning normality (although she had forgotten what that looked like). It worked. The teacher seemed to pay no notice. *See, no one cares.*

Claire had had a difficult year. The more she tried to 'persevere' the harder things became. It was the day before her tenth birthday when things really kicked off. Her Dad was late picking her up from school. He was in a foul mood. She wanted to tell him about her day - the project on the First World War and how food was rationed – but he only responded with half words like 'uh-hum' or 'oh'. It was clear he wasn't listening and so she decided to curtail it, '... and in the end, everyone died of starvation.' She looked up to see his reaction, but there was none. She half expected him to say, 'That's nice,' but he didn't.

Ten minutes later they were home. Mum wasn't there. As she climbed the stairs to her room, she could sense something was wrong. It was a couple of days later that she found out what had happened. Her mum had been diagnosed with stage two cancer and decided to move in with her sister, saying her being at home would be too much of a strain on the family. Claire suspected the reality was more to do with her not having Dad hanging around Mum's neck. He would always fuss over her and when she had enough, she'd scream at him: 'Give me some space, you moron!' That would push him away for a day or two, but then he'd be back again. He'd be offering to get her dinner, iron her clothes or do some other chore. Then, whenever she started to do some cleaning or washing, he'd jump in and try and take over.

Claire decided to hide in the art store cupboard. A year three teacher, one day, called her over and asked her to help carry some materials back to her classroom. As she was being loaded up, she quickly looked around the cupboard – which in fact was more like a room - noting where the switch was and the fact that there was no lock on the door. This would be a perfect hiding place she thought at the time. That time had now come.

She sandwiched herself on the floor between the shelves of coloured A4 paper and the rolls of display backing paper, near the far end. The room was big enough for a bed and, for a few moments, she imagined having her own room in the corner of the school, with its own sink, cooker and washing machine. That's all she'd need. She could fend for herself.

Claire was now feeling calmer. She realised her initial thoughts of running away were impractical. All she needed was space; her own space. The art cupboard seemed to wrap its arms around her, and she sensed something profound. She couldn't explain it at the time, but she knew this was a place she'd need to come back to. Yes, when she was in a better frame of mind. This could be her refuge. Somewhere no one else knew about.

An old wooden box lay just across from her. She reached over and lifted the lid. It was empty and judging by the film of dust, with her fingerprints now freshly implanted on it, she realised that it was no longer used. This would be her box. *Tomorrow, I'll get some provisions: a torch, a packet of Haribo sweets and other banned treats, an Argos catalogue and….* Claire realised she was smiling. Whatever had caused her rage was now forgotten. She picked herself up and decided to get back to class and face the music.

It was lunchtime and she could hear the other children outside playing. She found her teacher, Miss Harper, sitting by her desk, tucking into a sandwich.

‘I’m sorry Miss, I don’t know what came over me,’ Claire spluttered.

‘That’s ok,’ replied the teacher. ‘Come over here and take a seat.’

Miss Harper didn’t seem at all angry and this confused Claire.

‘You can spend your lunchtime here if you want.’

She passed Claire a book: *Times Like These* by Harold Winter. She started reading, but her mind soon drifted.

The rest of the afternoon went quickly. She was told that she should not make her own way home, as her dad would be collecting her. Apparently, the head teacher wanted to speak to him.

When Dad came out the head teacher’s office, he looked at Claire with a sympathetic smile. ‘Okay poppet, let’s go.’

She couldn’t work out why everyone was being so nice, considering what she’d done. At home, her dad tried to speak to her, but this time it was her turn to feign interest. Claire's mind just kept thinking about the Art Cupboard. *I need to give it a name. My Special Place? Too corny. Hideout? No, it sounds like something from the Famous Five series.* She then thought about the events which brought her there: the computer being smashed on the floor; the girl who kept nudging her whilst she was trying to work and Eric, the boy who thought it was funny to cuss her mum - something about being fat.

Eric was the class clown. He never did well in tests and Claire reckoned this was the reason why he spent his time bothering other children. His cusses never made sense anyway. She didn't care for him really, nor did anyone else, apart from Guy and Rory, who were his 'sheep'. They'd laugh even if the fire alarm went off.

Brainless! Mum was never fat. Claire's mum had been a model once and her looks never left her - that is until the cancer took its hold. Even after her hair fell out, if you looked closely, you could still see the beauty in her blue eyes and her smile - like the moon's crescent, not overbearing, full of grace and charm. *Idiot boy, cussing my mum like that.*

Claire decided on 'Solace'. She remembered reading it once in an extract from Charles Dickens. It meant 'comfort or consolation in a time of great distress or sadness'. She started to pack her school bag, something her mum always told her do. 'Make sure your bag's packed for tomorrow,' she'd say. Claire would look on her bedroom table to see if there was anything, like a stray pencil that she could just slide into her bag, then shout downstairs, 'Yes Mum.' One time she emptied her bag and found a handful of pencils, pens, rubbers and other random items like an old hairband and a Fruittella sweet still in its wrapper. This time she packed her bag with much deliberation: *Now, what can I take with me to Solace?*

Claire came into school, with her bag full. She was surprised at how much all the items weighed. She decided to ask Miss Harper if she could visit the toilet before registration. That would give her a chance to unload everything into her new room. She had thought it all out. In the side pouch she had a wet cloth, which she took out first. She carefully wiped the box; its top, sides and then underneath. She soon realised that this box simply wouldn't hold everything, so, as she took out the rest of the items, she decided which ones she would keep: The Argos catalogue: *Too big.* The Cadbury's chocolate bar, which she had found at the back of the fridge: *Box it.* The notebook and pen: *Box.* The plastic model of a snail: *Silly.* The silver cross her mum gave her just before she died: *Box.* The book Miss Harper had lent her: *Box.* The torch: *Too big, besides it needs batteries.* Her teddy bear: *No, I'm too old for that now.*

The bell rang and Claire suddenly realised she'd been gone too long. She quickly put the discarded items back in her bag and returned to class. Miss Harper was shouting at Eric whilst the rest of the class waited patiently in line. Fortunately, she didn't notice Claire's prolonged 'toilet visit'. Eric had been a good distraction. *He had his uses!*

The day went slowly. Claire kept looking for an opportunity to return to Solace. She offered to take the register to the office, but the teacher gave it to her assistant instead. At lunchtime, it was raining, and the class had to stay in their room.

A few days passed and every attempt to reach Solace was thwarted. The only other option was to be parked.

Two:

Ticket to Solace

Claire wasn't a violent person, apart from when she was in a rage. She racked her brain to think what non-violent offense she could commit that would merit a 'parking'. She could swear, but this was not becoming of her. Besides, Eric swore from time to time, and he would never be parked for it. She looked at Miss Harper and thought: *What if I were rude to her? This would surely get me sent out.* Claire leant forward at her desk, listening intently to her teacher, waiting for her cue.

'This afternoon, class, we will be looking at the British Isles. Who knows what countries make up the British Isles?'

She listened to her classmates as they each gave their answers. One girl then said, 'Miss, Poland too.'

'No Miss,' Claire interjected. 'Is Jennifer really that stupid -'

Her teacher cut her short. 'Claire, stop that right now!'

'Stop what, Miss?'

'Your rudeness.'

'You're rude,' Claire quickly replied, hoping that this would be enough for her to be sent out.

'Claire, I'd advise you calm down,' the teacher bellowed back. Claire wanted to stay in control, but she couldn't stop what was stirring inside her. Being told to 'calm down' seemed to ignite her anger. She wanted to swear. She wanted to grab something and throw it. *Who are you to tell me what to do*? *Who are you little Miss Harper?*

Events quickly turned. Claire remembered shouting an expletive at the teacher then throwing something, possibly a book. She was now standing outside the classroom. She looked at her hand and the piece of paper clenched in it.

Yes. My ticket to Solace. In the rush to get Claire out of her class, the teacher had not even bothered to fill in the rest of the slip.

Claire smiled. She never understood why children who couldn't be trusted inside the class, would get slips and then be trusted to take themselves to the designated parking class. In fact, she found the whole notion of parking quite amusing. It seemed benign. No one would tell you off and the offence would soon be forgotten. She remembered her dad telling her stories of how he'd be sent to stand outside the head teacher's office, where he'd have to wait for what seemed an eternity, get a telling off and even be excluded. This parking was like moving your car from one side of those vast shopping centres (the ones they always seem to give fancy names, like Green Lakes) to the other end. This way you could buy your groceries at Waitrose and then drive to where the cinemas and restaurants were located.

Claire walked past 5J, down the stairs, took a left and then looked up and down the corridor. She noticed that her rage had lifted. Solace seemed to have this effect. The mixed and distorted colours of rage all of a sudden seem to settle, like oil sitting calmly on the surface of water, its colours harmonised into the bands of a rainbow: something once ugly, now ordered and full of beauty.

She sat down, looking at her box. She reached for her mum's necklace and turned it over in her hand. Her finger ran over the shape of the cross. Its cold, yet smooth surface made her feel close to her mum. *Why did you have to leave me?* She laid it to her side, arranging the chain neatly so that it snaked like an s-shape. The box's lid was open, and she spotted the book her teacher had given her. She remembered pretending to read it the day she trashed the computer screen. Picking it up she turned to the back cover and read:

A story that takes you to different worlds: an adventure that will forever change you. Harold Winter has the ability to take the normal and make it bizarre. Each event is laced with intrigue which unravels itself, so that what was strange now seems normal and the resulting effect leaves the reader enlightened. Enjoy the journey as you enter *Times Like These*.

Interesting. Claire returned to the front cover: it was a picture of a boat on a lake, surrounded by mountains. The sun was off to the side at about quarter mast, the water catching its light, sparkling like jewels.

Chapter 1: Gathering crows

One by one they flew down into position, like a well-rehearsed dance. What happened next was not a dance though. The discarded brown bag lay temptingly open, but without upturning it no one would know what was inside. The first crow stepped forward and took a peck, quickly followed by the second who caused a slight tear, then like a firework exploding in the sky all five birds set upon it, wings raised, flapping and their voices tumultuously screeching at each other. Whatever the prize, they seemed to know it was worth the fight. The crows began to turn on each other in this voracious battle screaming all the more - no one wanting to lose whatever lay inside.

Turning back to the front cover, Claire pondered what fighting crows had to do with a setting sun on still lake. She read on: There was a sixth crow, sitting in the shadows and whilst his associates battled on, he came forward and seeing a clear path, walked straight up to the bag, grabbed its contents and with a skip and hop was off. The story intrigued her. One by one each crow morphed into a human. They had names and characters and they were all crooks – even the sixth crow. His name was Toby. Toby was shy and unassuming, so much so that his colleagues often forgot him. They called themselves the Fabulous Five. Toby called himself Sixth Sense:

Toby watched his five associates as they sat around the table, drinks in hand, making small talk - laughing at the slightest thing. 'Evening all,' he greeted as he sat down with his diet coke. He was not one for alcohol. He knew it would affect his ability to operate with stealth and cunning. 'Oh Toby, how's it been going?' one offered, but before he had a chance to reply, they'd all returned to their idle chatter.

The story began to unfold. They were planning to rob the local post office. They'd discussed the best time and how they would operate. Toby would be a lookout. Already, he knew in his own mind what this meant. He would be watching them! £100,000, or whatever the stake turned out to be, shared six ways would be far less than the £100,000. Toby knew each of their weaknesses and as they discussed their plans, he did his own planning.

To cut a long story short (as Claire's dad would often say), the robbery went ahead. Crow one left the money bags in the car; crow two tripped on the curb taking crow three down with him; crow four and five made it inside, shouting at the cashier to hand over the money, but in their panic forgot to put their hoods up to disguise their faces. Grabbing the money, they smothered it close to their chests and made for the exit. Toby was meant to be in the car ready to drive them all off and although the car door was open, it was empty – no Toby, no key! They looked at each other in disbelief. Toby appeared with the moneybags and took over. He instructed crows four and five to place the money in the bags (which he now possessed) and gave the key to crow one. 'Let's go!' he ordered. They all jumped in the car and it sped off. Toby watched coolly as it turned the first corner.

'Foolish Five,' he chuckled to himself. With that he morphed back into his animal form and flew off.

Claire liked this story. Toby was so smooth - calculating and confident. She remembered something her mum used to say to her: *The race is not to the swift or strong but to those who endure to the end.*

Time had passed and Claire realised that a clock would be a good thing to keep in her box. She placed the book and necklace back in their place, closed the lid, tapping its top as if to say: 'Thank you.' Opening Solace's door slightly she checked to see if the corridor was clear. She made her way back upstairs and decided it would be smart to check into 5J with her parking slip – it's what Toby would have done. Thirty minutes later, one of her classmates appeared asking for her to return to class. It was home time already. She couldn't believe the whole afternoon had gone so quickly.

Claire realised that if Solace were to be her place of refuge, she would need to find a way of spending time there each day. She believed the room had a way of refreshing her soul. She didn’t really know how. It wasn’t something religious. It was something more tangible. Only time would tell.

Three:

Silence

The rest of the week passed without any further drama, but Claire became restless. She spent half her time listening to the teacher and half the time thinking about how she could re-visit Solace. She actually became good at it – she was able to filter out most of the ‘chat’ and pick out the key teaching points, so that if she was ever put on the spot, she’d be able to give a half sensible answer.

It was Friday afternoon, Golden Time, and activities were relaxed. The teacher said this was a reward. Claire believed it was because the teacher was exhausted, that it was her ‘time out’; time to unwind and slide into the weekend.

Claire took a book from the book corner, wishing she had *Times Like These*. As she pretended to read, her mind focused in on this idea that she could somehow spend each day visiting Solace.

'...and don't forget to bring your forms in for breakfast club next week,' Miss concluded.

That's it. Breakfast club. Perfect.

'Miss, I don't think I've got a form,' Claire blurted out, forgetting to raise her hand. Miss Harper ignored this misdemeanour and told her to collect one from reception on her way out. Claire didn't know how the breakfast club would be her season ticket to Solace, but she had the weekend to figure it out. Once dismissed, she took a detour, collected *Times Like These* and then made her way to the reception desk.

* * *

Dad glanced at the form, saying, 'Mmm, that looks good,' signed it, and then gave it back. *If only things would be that simple. Maybe I should ask him for a hundred pounds!*

'So, I'm going to leave here at seven in the morning?' she asked, but really it was a statement.

'Yeah, that's fine sweetie,' he said looking up from his paper. Claire wondered how much of the paper he actually read, as he seemed to be able to turn each page in a matter of seconds - mind you, there were lots of pictures.

Monday morning soon came, and Claire left as arranged at seven on the dot. Dad was upstairs shaving and she gave her customary 'Byeee!' as she shut the door.

The school gate was open, and the playground was empty. It all very felt very strange. Claire didn't even know where the breakfast club was located, but she knew where Solace was. Walking through the school building she had to question herself. It did not feel like school at all. She could hear a low humming further down the corridor, which she imagined was one of the cleaners vacuuming. *This is so easy.*

Claire opened the door to the art cupboard. It was dark. She had been used to having the light from the small window at the end of the room and since it was winter, hardly any light was coming in. Sitting down, she reached into her bag and took out the small alarm clock that she'd bought from the pound shop over the weekend.

Feeling in the box, she found *Times Like These*. She looked at the cover again, but in the dark it seemed more like a menacing shadow encroaching on open field, very different from the peaceful lake it was meant to show. Turning to chapter two she could just about make out the title: Still waters. To read on was hopeless. She decided she'd visit the pound shop on the way home and get some batteries for her torch. There was just enough room left in the box for it.

The room was quiet. The humming she heard earlier had stopped. There was nothing apart from the thoughts running around inside her head. She suddenly realised that she wasn't happy. A year ago, her mum had died, and this was the first time she had stopped to think about how she felt. She didn't like it and the longer she sat there, the deeper the thoughts became. She longed for light to break through the window or at least for the sound of someone in the corridor outside, so she wouldn't feel so alone.

'Why did you have to die?' she spoke out as if expecting a reply. 'Why, why, why …,' she repeated as she lowered her head to her hands and started to cry.

The tears are like little boats, one by one bringing out the anguish from her troubled soul.

Claire lifted her head, disturbed by a sound outside. She reached for her clock: 07:50. The room was now filling with light. Something had happened there in Solace. A release. She couldn't understand it, but as she reached for the book and read the chapter title, 'Still Waters', it seemed to pull her in.

The moorhen frantically moved about her nest. The water was lapping inside and although it was designed to leak water back out, it wasn't doing it quickly enough. Bits of the nest were falling apart, with twigs drifting off into the water. She scuttled from one side to the other doing her best to repair it. The storm seemed unrelenting. She looked down at the seven eggs she'd been brooding over, wondering if any of them would survive. In fact, she decided that if things became worse, she'd concentrate on saving just one. She chose the one marked with red speckles and moved it to the centre of the nest.

Claire read on determined to finish the chapter before 8.30, giving her time to reach the 'breakfast club', sign in, grab a toast and then go to class at 8.45.

The moorhen morphed into a young and somewhat distressed woman, Jackie, who was at her wit's end.

She'd just received a letter, mostly written in red – a final notice requiring her to pay her rent or face the consequences. The prospect of being homeless threw her into a state of panic. She had three days to find £629. All she had left from the benefit money she had withdrawn on Monday, was £80.

The story continued, as she asked her family, neighbours, even the local church for money. Each declined, with their own sob story of financial woes. She decided to send the two older children off to their dad's, keeping her youngest close to her side. If she was made homeless, she felt she could manage with just the one. After many tears (from all four of them), she reviewed the situation. She would eat one meal a day, sharing it with her three-year-old. All the other bills would be put on hold. £80 would cover expenses for the week and the £629 for the rent would have to be …

Claire flicked the page over, desperate to find out how this poor woman would recover from the looming disaster. Jackie decided she would steal the money. She returned to the church and decided to snoop around. At the back she found a collection box. It was locked, but after a few yanks it suddenly gave way and flew open. Coins fell out and there were a few notes inside. She grabbed every one and then quickly departed. She felt no guilt, despite it being a church. She felt she was owed it. Someone in need.

It wasn't enough. She knew this even without counting it. Jackie continued visiting places where she felt she was owed and eventually collected what was required for the rent.

Still waters. Claire wondered at this strange title. The moorhen survived. Jackie kept her home, albeit for another month. Maybe it was about survival. *Stormy waters, still waters? Life is a cycle like that, I guess.*

Four:

Lunch Money

Claire made it to class, just finishing off her toast and jam as she walked through the door. The morning sessions were maths followed by grammar and then just before lunch, Miss Harper announced that they would be performing 'Oliver' for the end of year performance. Claire loved this play and, for some reason, became besotted with the idea of Artful Dodger, the wily pickpocket. Not that she wanted the part, but there was something about his stealth and cunningness that excited her. Claire's life was about to take an unexpected turn: Crow number six, Jackie the thief and now Claire the Dodger. It seemed like fate.

On Miss Harper's desk was a plastic bag for the children's weekly lunch money. *Thirty times £2 times five… £300!* Some children were on packed lunch and some had free school dinners, but Claire reckoned there would be at least £100 in there.

During the afternoon, Claire took her history book over to Miss Harper.

'Miss, can you read over what I've done?'

Miss read it, looked up and smiled: 'Claire, this is really good. Maybe you could add some key dates, but you have used some good descriptive language...'

Claire thanked Miss Harper and returned to her desk, clutching the bag of money, that she had lifted from the teacher's desk, close to her side. As soon as she sat down, she slid it into her tray and covered it with some loose worksheets. Her heart was beating furiously like a drum. Claire picked up her pen and pretended to write. She looked up hoping no one had noticed her guilt, but everyone was busy about their work. She replayed the whole episode to herself and a sense of satisfaction came over her: *I did it. Claire the Dodger did it!*

It wasn't until she got home and locked her bedroom door that she poured the money out. She counted it twice over and found that her visit to Miss Harper's desk had made her exactly £160. She counted it a third time. It wasn't that she doubted the total, more that she enjoyed the feel of all the different notes and coins filing through her fingers.

Miss Harper didn't mention the missing money, but she seemed perturbed over the following few days. Claire noticed, a week later, that Miss put the money in a draw once it had been collected, which was then locked.

Claire now had an established routine. She'd get up and be out of the house by 7am. Getting to school early allowed her to sneak off to Solace, where she would sit for a while; getting used to the silence she would wrestle with her thoughts. Then reaching for her book she'd read, leaving this world and entering another full of strange fantasies. These stories were like fables. Each seemed to have a message, although they weren't always clear. '

'Why would Miss give me this book?' she wondered to herself.

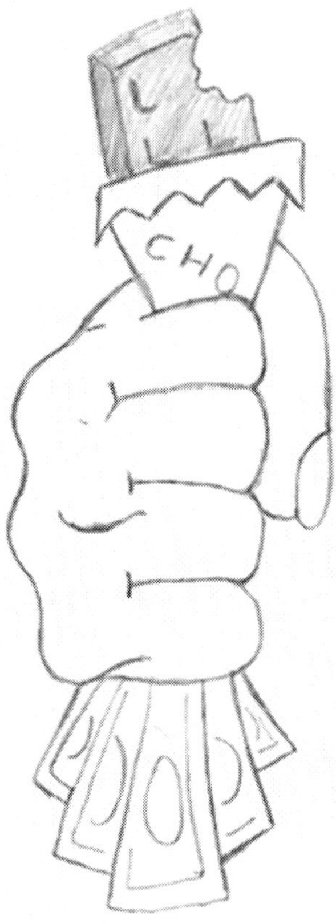
CHO

Five:

Easter Holidays

The end of term arrived and as Claire made her way home, she started to feel afraid. She wasn't sure what it was she was worried about. Most children relished the opportunity to be off school, but not Claire. Her dad had just got a new job, meaning he was hardly around. She had no siblings and her grandparents lived miles away. She also realised that spending time each morning in Solace had caused her to withdraw from her friends. Normally she'd have one or two friends she'd meet up with, to go shopping or do a sleep over. Mum would organise it. Claire's fear turned to anger.

She wasn't ready to go home. The prospect of loneliness sent a shiver through her body. She crossed the road and made a beeline for the local supermarket. It was larger than most – a super store. It had 24 aisles; she knew this because the milk was on the last aisle. That used to mystify her. The thing people needed the most, was the hardest to reach. Claire needed peace and it felt like a million miles away.

It was on the 23rd aisle that Claire stopped. The sign above her head read ‘Confectionery’. Her eyes were drawn to a large bar of chocolate and without any further thought she picked it up and walked towards the exit. Claire wanted to tempt fate and walked just as far as the security guard on the doors. She tore the wrapper back, broke a piece of chocolate off and popped it in her mouth. She looked up at the man, who was preoccupied with his TV monitors and then walked out. No alarms went off. No angry voices came shouting after her. She had just shop lifted and got away with it. She couldn’t believe it. She felt elated; every thought of loneliness had vanished.

Getting home, Claire climbed the stairs to her room. She threw her school bag down and reached into the corner, just behind her bed. Lifting the carpet up, she felt her hand under and pulled out the £160, which had been there for the last three weeks. She counted out the money and decided she would start a new hobby: collecting money. She had no need for it, but holding it made her feel alive. There were several ten-pound notes and she placed them together, making them all face the same way, with the Queen glancing to her right. She took the rest of the money, five-pound notes and various coins, placed them in her pocket and made her way back outside. Finding the nearest corner shop, she approached the shopkeeper and asked for them to be changed into ten-pound notes. He obliged and on returning home she placed them with the others: Sixteen in total. She then decided she wanted twenty, a nice round number. With that she went into her dad's room. He had left the door open, which used to annoy her, as it was always in a mess: his unmade bed, clothes on the floor and abandoned cups and plates with remains of whatever in. This time the room invited, rather than repelled her.

Claire started to sift through her dad's stuff. She felt apprehensive, not knowing what she'd find. She lifted papers, opened draws and even looked inside his wardrobe, checking pockets, but alas, there was not a penny to be found. *This is hopeless. He must have something of value!* Claire walked back to the door, checking the room once more to ensure nothing looked out of place. *The mess looks the same.* She wanted to shut the door, as if to remind herself never to enter again, but decided that she didn't want to give any hint of her troubling his room.

Entering the front room, Claire slumped in her dad's chair, picked up the remote and started flicking through the channels. The chair sunk in the middle. No one else was allowed to sit in it, and now she had tried it, she wondered why anyone else would want to sit in it. It was angled so that it half faced the TV and half faced the display cabinet at the far end of the room. *That's it!* Claire jumped up and walked over to the cabinet. Opening the glass door, she reached past the naff ornaments and picked up a small golden clock. She remembered her dad talking about it one day, something about a wedding gift from his company. *This must have some value.* She ran upstairs and placed it in her old plastic toy box, tucking it behind a collection of teddy bears and dolls from previous years. Claire returned to the front room and sat back in her usual chair.

When Dad came home, he went through his normal routines. Claire was watching him out of the corner of her eye. He hung his jacket on the stair post and kicked off his shoes, leaving them at the side by the front door. His keys and phone clunked as they were placed on the table in the hall and then he went directly to the kitchen. Claire closed her eyes and imagined him as he took out a beer from the fridge. Seconds later he was with her in the front room, sinking into his chair. 'Hello sweetie, what are you doing down here?' Claire asked herself the same question, realising she had no cause to be there. The TV was off, and she had no book or tablet to entertain her.

'We broke up today,' she responded, hoping he'd forgotten his question.

'That's nice, Easter holidays?'

'Yep … two weeks … just thinking what I can do.'

Flicking on the TV, Dad declared: 'Let's see what's going on in the world.'

This was another one of his routines … watching the News at Six. He'd watch it, flick the channels a few times and then watch it again at seven o'clock, on a different channel, even though it was the same news all over again.

Claire sat there for what seemed an eternity, watching TV and making small talk with her dad. What she really wanted to see was whether he'd noticed the clock had gone. She decided, just as the News at Ten was starting, that she'd ask him outright.

'Dad, what are those ornaments supposed to be in the cabinet?' Dad looked up and paused for a few moments. Claire held her breath. Her heart was beating hard and her mind was racing: *What if he notices? I could say I took it upstairs to find a battery for it …*

'I don't know really; it was a little hobby of your mum's. One day I'll sort them out. Maybe you could help me choose one or two to keep. The rest could go to charity.'

'Sounds like a plan,' Claire responded, although she was angry that he would even consider getting rid of anything of mum's.

With that she got up and went upstairs. She'd had dinner before Dad came home - he never ate in the evening and he never made anything for her. *Lazybones of a dad!*

Six:

Anger Boils

That night, Claire stayed up late. The silence crept up on her, but this time it was like the tide of the sea. Her emotions increased with every incoming wave, each bringing a new set of negative thoughts. If *I were to vanish tomorrow, Dad wouldn't even notice. In fact, no one would notice.* Claire's anger was being stirred and there was no outlet. Overwhelming loneliness crowded her, like darkness trying to extinguish the last flames of a candle. Tears welled up in her eyes and she quietly sobbed. *I hate Dad. What has he ever done for me?* Moments later she was asleep.

When the morning came, Claire wasted no time. She washed and dressed. Skipping breakfast, she retrieved the clock from the toy box, wrapped it in newspaper and placed it in her backpack. Dad had already left for work; his door left open with a new mess arranged around the room.

Cash Converters was a new shop in town, and she had often passed it. This time she would go in. She went up to the counter and placed the clock on it. 'How much?' she demanded. The woman looked at her and Claire tried to avoid eye contact.

'How old are you?' she asked.

'My dad needs the money. He's ill at home and I'm his carer.'

'I'll give you twenty' the woman responded and handed over 2 ten-pound notes. Claire hesitated. She was sure it was worth more and besides she needed another forty pounds to complete her collection.

'Dad said I shouldn't accept less than forty,' Claire said, this time making eye contact. 'He's really ill and we've got bills to pay.' The woman hesitated and then reaching back into the till, she handed Claire three ten-pound notes, saying that was the best she could do. Claire took it, glad to make the extra ten, and was then back on the high street.

£10 more and I'll have £200. She looked up and down the street wondering how she could chance upon some more money. *Pity seems to work a treat.*

With that thought she sat on a bench, next to an old lady and then started to cry.

'What's the matter, poppet?' the lady enquired.

'My dad will kill me,' Claire replied. 'He gave me £10 to buy his groceries and now I've gone and lost it.'

'I'm his carer,' she added.

Without delay, the lady reached into her bag opened her purse and pulled out a folded ten-pound note. Claire decided it didn't matter that it was creased: this was number twenty. Mission complete. She smiled at the lady and thanked her, wiping away the crocodile tears. Getting up, Claire felt surprised at how easily she could manipulate people.

The rest of the holidays passed, but with each day, her sadness grew. Whilst the stealing was exciting, it wasn't enough to quell the anger and rage she felt inside. Claire wondered where this would end.

Seven:

New Girl

Claire never had a problem going to school, but for some reason the thought of getting out of bed became like a heavy weight that travelled through her whole body. She managed to sit up but then flopped straight back down. *Just ten more minutes.*

A noise downstairs startled her, and she realised it was her dad leaving for work. She looked over at her bedside clock and was surprised to see it read 08:10. She had time to get ready but knew she wouldn't make it to Solace.

Walking into the school gates, she observed her classmates as they formed their little groups, exchanging stories of their holidays. Claire didn't want to talk to anyone and held back, standing by the fence, clutching her bag. She wanted the day to end. The bell rang and she made her way over to the class line. Once in the class, the teacher promptly got everyone reading. Claire took a random book from the book corner and flicked through it looking at the pictures.

'Right class,' Miss Harper announced. 'We have a new student with us today … everyone say hello to Aliya.' The class duly responded with 'Hi's' and 'Hello's'.

'Aliya is from Jamaica. She only arrived here two days ago, isn't that right?' she asked, looking at the new girl. Her black hair was different from the rest of the girls in the class: neatly plaited, just reaching below her shoulders and held back with a shiny black headband. She looked shy, but there was something Claire noticed in her eyes, a look of determination. It drew her attention.

'Yes Miss,' Aliya responded.

The teacher then asked her to share a little about herself and Aliya proceeded to talk about the town she lived in, how it was small, and most people didn't own cars. She talked about her school. Her class had 35 children who stayed in the same room all day, apart from when they had break. It was very hot, and they would have a 'sleep break' in the middle of the afternoon. She missed her friends.

Aliya spoke well. Her accent had a slight twang. She didn't smile, but there was something about her that Claire liked – her calmness.

At break time, Claire decided she would befriend Aliya. She was tired of her old friends and felt they judged her, especially after the episode of her smashing of the computer screen. Aliya was happy to have someone to talk to. She shared about how her mum had recently passed away, knocked over by a speeding car that had veered off the road. Within a week of the funeral, she was told to pack all her clothes. Unaware of what was happening, her uncle drove her to the airport. He explained that she would be going to England to stay with her grandmother. She'd never met her gran and only knew her by the placard held up as she came out of Gatwick Airport. Aliya said that her gran had told her 'providence is the hand that will lead her'. Claire didn't know what this meant, but she liked how it sounded. *Providence will lead me. Providence will lead me.* Claire said it over as if its words had a power that could save her.

Claire shared briefly about how her mum had passed away from cancer a year ago and that it was just her and her dad.

Returning home that day, Claire had forgotten all her grief. Her rage had ceased to boil and now gently simmered in the background. Her new friend had filled a gap and she hoped it would last. The next day she got up with the alarm, washed, dressed and left the house with her customary 'bye'. She walked with purpose, wanting to find out more about her new friend Aliya.

Claire stayed at breakfast club for its entirety. Most children played outside, whilst some stayed inside to play board games. She decided to have a game of draughts with one of the year five children. She won. *Today is going to be a good day.*

Register was called. Everyone was present apart from Aliya. Claire looked around the class, wondering where she might be, but there was no sign of her. The day began with Maths practice. They were doing arithmetic, a subject she enjoyed. She finished within the twenty minutes allotted time and then looked up, scouring the room again to see if Aliya had magically appeared. The day continued and every time someone came through the door, a support teacher or another pupil with a message for Miss Harper, Claire turned to see...but there was no Aliya.

TIMES LIKE
THESE

Eight:

Exclusion

At lunchtime Claire decided to visit Solace. She had almost forgotten the room existed, but the sadness of not seeing her new friend drew her there. No one saw her as she sneaked down the corridor, opened the door of the art cupboard and slipped inside. She went over to the corner where her box sat waiting, opened it and took out *Times Like These*:

Chapter 3: Run for Your Life

He was the most handsome of squirrels. Standing tall on his hind legs he looked about him. Squirrels had to be alert, particularly first thing in the morning during dog walking hours. He noted the tree to his right, and with no dogs or their human companions in sight, he started digging the ground. His prize was to be hidden until an opportune time. Sam stopped. It wasn't that he heard anything, but he could sense danger.

The story continued. Sam was a squirrel, but in the strange parallel world the book created, he was also a soldier in the First World War. Claire had remembered studying about this war and the horrors of the trenches. Sam was stuck in No Man's Land. His battalion had been ordered over the parapet and one by one his comrades had been struck down. He had tripped on some barbed wire and as he lay on the ground, fear seized him. He knew if he was to get up the Huns would pick him off too. The line between life and death was so thin he became confused as to which realm he stood – or lay in as the case was. Maybe he was already dead. The story jumped back to that of the squirrel. The dog was fast approaching and as Sam ran to the tree, he felt himself yanked back. He gathered himself and started to run again. Pain was searing through his body, but he knew he had to make it to the tree and clamber up out of reach. Sam made it, and as he rested on one of the branches, he looked down. The dog was walking off, resigned to losing the chase, head hung low. He then examined his behind to see what damage had been caused and to his shock, the last third of his tail was missing. Sam hopped along the branch some more but felt odd. He slipped and his claws stuck fast into the tree's bark. He felt dizzy, but his head wasn't hurting. His balance was hampered, and he realised that his damaged tail was causing this.

The explosion was so loud it left a ringing in Sam's ear. He also felt something hard whack his leg. In a state of confusion, he decided that if he laid there any longer, he would surely die. He noticed some soldiers starting to retreat. He could see the trenches behind him and reckoned that if he made a run for it, he could make it back. He lifted himself into a crouched position and then counted down: *five, four, three, two, one … go!* And with that he stood and lurched forward. As he tried to place his left leg in front of his right, he simply stumbled back to the ground. He tried again with the same result. Looking down he saw that his left leg, from above the knee down, was not there.

Despair is life's greatest enemy. Both the squirrel and the soldier were faced with a life-changing situation. Both had to continue, although death seemed like an easy way out. The story concluded with both deciding to make the most of it. The squirrel groomed his tail and even though he knew he would have to be careful in future, he still held his head high. The soldier made it back to the trenches – it took him what must have been an hour to crawl back and throw himself over. From there he was taken to the makeshift hospital and then back to England to be rehabilitated. The war was over, but his battle continued. In time, he was able to get about. He found a simple job at the local factory and there met the love of his life. Despair had lost, its head held low, returning to the darkness from where it had come.

Claire had enjoyed this story. It filled her with hope. Maybe her troubles would leave her one day. Maybe she could hold her head high and walk with pride. Sadly though, that day was still far off.

* * *

Back in class, Miss Harper had demonstrated how to use colours to complement each other and the children were given a task to paint any object of their choice experimenting with colours. Everything was going well. Claire wasn't the greatest artist, but she loved experimenting. She looked at her painting, holding it up to admire. She imagined the golden colours of a Jamaican beach, with the blue sea tinted with the colours of the sun as it set on the horizon. She smiled and then thought of Aliya. Claire decided she would give the picture to her, and if for any reason she wasn't in school the next day, she'd ask her teacher to send it to her.

Eric was sitting opposite, and he was starting to laugh with the boy next to him. Then looking up at Claire, the following events seemed to play out in slow motion. The back of his hand lifted up and knocked the cup of water used to wash out the brushes. It tilted over towards Claire and water began to flow out. It made its way directly towards Claire's work. Claire froze in shock. She could hear other children pushing their chairs back with a collective gasp, some clutching their work. The water ran straight over the sky, then over the red tinted sea and then onto the golden beach, carrying all the colours with it. It was as if a knife had sliced right through her work, drawing a line of blood.

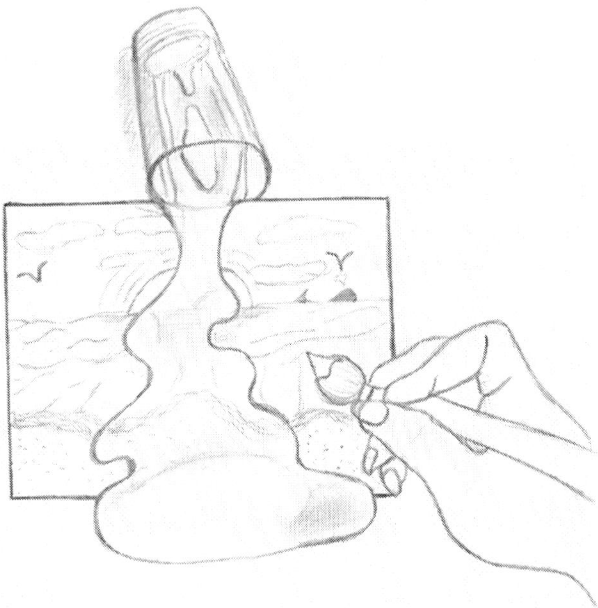

The water continued over the edge of her desk and down onto her skirt. She could feel the dampness going through to her legs. At the same time, she could feel a bubbling of rage lifting inside. She looked back at Eric, who was still laughing, and then screamed. The rest of the events were a haze. She knew she had lost it and now found herself in the head teacher's office sobbing uncontrollably.

Her dad was called in and this time there were no sympathetic smiles to console her. Claire had been given a three-day exclusion. Dad was shouting at her, telling her to get a grip. Claire shouted back telling him to leave her alone.

'I'm better off without you. It should have been you. Why did cancer take my mum? I wish you were dead!' Claire shot out of the room, ran upstairs and slammed the door as hard as she could. Claire threw herself onto her bed and found herself shaking. She couldn't believe what she had just said. It was full of venom. She didn't mean it, but it was the only way she could stop her dad from going on.

Dad was wounded. He kept quiet around the house and the only time he spoke was to call Claire down for meals. The atmosphere was tense. When they passed each other around the house, they both tried to smile at each other. It was awkward. Claire preferred it this way.

The three-day exclusion had run its course as the weekend drew to an end. Claire decided she needed a plan for her return to school. She found a piece of paper and wrote on it:

How to survive:

1) Go to Solace each morning
2) Have one friend (Aliya)
3) Keep out of Eric's way
4) Don't rise to provocations (Eric!)

Monday morning soon came, and Claire found herself back in Solace. She had now created a routine. The days were getting longer, and this offered the room more light, but she was still glad for the torch. She read from *Times Like These* and took time to reflect on each story. Some spoke to her, others didn't. Some confused her and she wondered whether they were encouraging bad behaviour, like that of Toby, the sixth crow, in Chapter 1. Nonetheless she enjoyed reading them. It was like a moral compass, even though sometimes it pointed in the wrong direction. They gave Claire a sense of being and purpose. Sometimes in Solace, Claire would take out her mum's necklace and thread it through her fingers trying to remember times spent together. When she felt ready, she would place everything back in the box then make her way to breakfast club, where she would sit in the games corner and wait for someone to join her for a game of draughts or snakes and ladders.

Aliya was at school and when they caught up at break time, Claire shared about the events of the previous days. Aliya was touched by the painting intended for her and agreed with Claire that Eric was a nuisance. They pledged they would avoid him like the plague. Being on side with Aliya made Claire feel alive again – a feeling she had lost when her mum passed away. Although they were different from each other, their circumstances drew them together.

Nine:

Normality

Exam season was upon them and lessons had become boring. If it wasn't maths, then it was writing, grammar or spelling. The only thing that broke this monotony was the assemblies (which used to be boring but were now a welcome break from studying) and the P.E. lessons on Wednesday afternoons. Aliya was amazing at every sporting activity. She was agile and could run as fast as the boys. She generally kept quiet, unless she was with Claire. Her Gran had told her to keep her head down and be humble. This seemed to work well for Aliya. No one bothered her. Claire watched her during lessons and realised she was particularly bright. Once, Claire noted how Aliya had finished a maths paper in half the allotted time and then just went through it slowly at the end so that people would think she was still working. She scored 38 out of 40. Claire wondered if she'd actually deliberately made mistakes so as to not get 100%.

The week before the exams, Miss Harper asked the class to bring in money for the end of year trip. Hearing the word money, Claire instinctively sat up. It had triggered a thirst in her. She visualised the 20 ten-pound notes at home, neatly placed in a plastic zip up bag, still hidden under the carpet. She remembered the folded one the old lady had given her in pity. She later ironed it, using one of Dad's clean hankies – she remembered Mum using a sheet sometimes when ironing, to stop it burning the item.

Exam week came and went, and children started to bring in their trip money. As Miss Harper collected it, she placed it in her lock up draw. The key was then placed in her handbag, which she kept by her at all times. The only way Claire could add to her collection was to intercept the money before it reached Miss Harper. She had to act quickly.

The next day, Claire left Solace early, only half reading a story. She spent some time in the breakfast club and then went to the cage. This is where the boys would play football. She watched them. They chased the ball around like kittens playing with a ball of wool. To the side, she could see where they had laid their coats and bags. She walked over, pushing some aside to make a little island, where she sat down. Looking up at the boys, she realised they were so engrossed in their game that she could easily riffle through their belongings without being noticed.

'Gooooal!' she heard one shout and the others ran over to congratulate him. The other team had their heads down. She picked up the first bag placing it on her lap and calmly opened it. Shifting the books around, she found an envelope. It had 'Trip Money' written on it. *Jackpot!* She folded it in half and placed it into the front of her own bag. Before the bell had rung, Claire had managed to get through five bags, finding money in three of them.

On the way home later that day, she stopped at the newsagent and changed some of the money into tens. She now had 26 notes. As the week progressed, Claire managed to raise another £140, making it 40 notes. The spout of thefts had come to the head teacher's notice and a 'special assembly' was held to challenge the thief to give himself up. Claire smiled to herself thinking why they would assume the thief was a 'he'.

Claire wasn't so down: she had a friend to pass each day with; her ten-pound note collection was doing well; her dad kept out of her way; Eric had found someone else to bother; and the time each morning in Solace seemed to help.

Rummaging around in her desk draw at home, Claire soon found what she was looking for – the calendar her nan had bought her for Christmas. She tore off the first five pages and then held it up in front of her. It had pictures of flowers around the border, but she decided she could ignore them. It was the empty slots with each day's number that demanded her interest. She'd never used a calendar before. She drew a smiley face on a small round piece of card and with a piece of Blu Tack, placed it on today's date. She then found some highlighters and decided to mark off the days she had left at school in florescent yellow. Counting them, she found that there were only 23 more days before finishing her primary education. This surprised her. She started thinking about how she would spend them. Yes, there was the school play, in which she had a small part, then there was the school trip, the school disco and graduation. She marked each off putting a question mark next to the disco and graduation. She decided she'd only go to the disco if Aliya was going and as for the graduation, she couldn't see the point – her mum wouldn't be there and as for her dad …

Strangely, filling in the calendar gave Claire a sense of purpose. Her life started to have some form of structure. She decided it would be a bad idea to steal anymore at school and she would continue to stay calm, even if provoked. She couldn't afford to be excluded again. This was for Aliya. She felt she had to make the most of the little time left at school to build the friendship. After all, she needed a friend to spend time with over the six-week summer holiday. She then took out the ten-pound notes. There were still 40 there and she wrote the number next to the smiley face on the calendar.

Ten:

Scamming

The weekend came and Claire decided to try the 'poor little girl' scam again. This time she didn't feel at ease. It wasn't spontaneous like before and the planning of it made her feel nervous. She went to the pedestrianised part of town and started to walk along its length, looking casually into the shop windows. A police officer passed her and she looked down, feeling guilty. Reaching the end of the pedestrianised area, she turned around and decided she would sit on the first bench she spotted with someone on it.

The man was middle aged, bald, with broad shoulders. He didn't look at all friendly, but Claire stuck to her decision. She sat at the opposite end of the bench, squashed up against the arm. She looked over at the man who seemed distant. If she was going to get this £10 she knew she'd have to be authentic and with that she pushed her nerves aside and started to sob. It was more of a sniffle with sharp intakes of breath. She did it a few times, waiting for the man to respond, but nothing! Claire now felt like crying for real and so the next part seemed to come more easily. She gave a little yelp and then started to cry. This time it was louder. Her voice jittered out the sobs. *Surely he will hear me.* A young lady with a shopping bag came over and the man rose to his feet.

'What's wrong with her?' she enquired.

'I don't know,' he responded, 'She just sat down and started crying.'

The lady turned her attention to Claire. She was pretty, with long dark hair and neatly cut eyebrows, making her face seem petite.

'What's the matter love?' she asked.

This was Claire's cue: she spun her story as before. Then, with £10 delivered firmly in her hand, Claire thanked the woman - more because she was released from the embarrassment of sitting sobbing next to the bald man, than for receiving the £10. Tucking the money into her jean's pocket, she got up and then proceeded to the next bench where she repeated the same tactic. It worked. She spotted the police officer and this time she sensed he was actually watching her. Being careful, she waited a few minutes and then got up, walked a little further and sat down at the third bench. Looking up and down, noticing the police officer was nowhere to be seen she repeated her antics. With £30 now tucked in her jeans' pocket she decided to call it a day. She had been lucky so far. She didn't want to push it, reasoning that someone would eventually spot her, wondering why the same girl was crying at different benches.

Walking home Claire felt disappointed. The excitement she experienced the first time she went out and sold her dad's carriage clock wasn't there. The spontaneity had gone. The daring and adrenalin was missing. She stopped, reached into her pocket and took out the £30. *I can do better than this.* She turned around and walked purposefully back into town. Up ahead was the gadget shop, at least that's what she called it. It had all the latest phones, computers and televisions. Gadgets weren't really her thing. She looked around and saw clusters of adults here and there. Some were gathered around a large screen with surround sound, as if they were in the cinema, each with their eyes glued to the screen. A salesman was busy chatting away, probably giving them all the specs, which seemed to go right over their transfixed heads.

Claire made her way over to where the mobile phones were. She picked up the first one but realised it was stuck to its cradle with a piece of security wire. Walking a little further along, she soon discovered they were all attached in this way. At the very end of the display unit, there was a 'new phone' - it was obvious due to all the advertising around it and the special glass top it was stuck to. This one she couldn't even pick up.

A sales assistant came over. He was young and enthusiastic. Claire reckoned he was new to the job and this became apparent as he struggled to give her the blurb about how many gigabytes it had and its internet connection speed. Claire finally asked, 'So, how much is it?'

'On a contract, it is ...'

Claire cut him short: 'How much is it without a contract?'

'£499,' he responded, pointing at the chart with all the tariffs and prices.

'Can I have a look at it please?' Claire asked looking directly into his eyes.

He hesitated and then said, 'Sure ... I'll be right back'. Claire's mind kicked into overdrive. How would she walk out of the shop with this new phone and not get stopped? She looked around again to see where the other shop assistants were. They were all seemed preoccupied with other customers. She then spied the exit, where a large security man stood. He had monitors in front of him, which he appeared to be studying.

The young assistant returned quicker than Claire had expected. He placed the box in front of her: 'You're the first person to see this phone,' he proudly announced. 'This will be our demonstration phone ... I had to cut the seal for you to have a look.' Claire carefully opened the box as if it were a Christmas present from her mum. Mum always bought nice presents. Dad usually got some cheap annual or sticker book or whatever else he could find at the last minute.

'Wow!' she exclaimed, 'It looks even better, fresh out of the box.'

How can I get him to leave?

'Do you have phone covers for it?' she enquired.

'Well, since this is new on the market, there is only one that will fit it. Would you like to see?'

'Sure,' Claire responded and with that he jumped up again to return to the storeroom. Claire had to think quickly. She looked up at the security man. He was now talking to a customer who had just entered the store. She looked back over to the storeroom door to see if the young assistant was returning and then, as if in a flash, she slipped the £499 phone into her jeans pocket. She picked up the box, sliding it shut, but something felt wrong. It was too light. She quickly looked about and wondered what she could put in there to act as a weight. Her heart was now beating double time, as she thought she would surely get caught. To her left she noticed another display board, with batteries hanging on it. This time without even checking to see what the security man was doing or where the young assistant was, she got up went over to the display and picked up a pack of six batteries. By the time she was back at the 'new phone' display she had already opened the box and taken them out. She placed four of them side by side in the phone box with two at the top like pillows on a bed. The young assistant returned, just as she slid the box back together.

'That was hard to find', he said, slightly out of breath.

'You know what,' Claire said, 'I don't think I like this phone after all'. She pushed the box towards the young assistant, who looked at her bemused. He picked it and was about to open it.

'I put it back, exactly how I found it', Claire quickly asserted, sealing the lie with her cutest smile. He smiled back. Lifting the box up, he held it for a few moments.

'Well if you change your mind, feel free to come back'. With that, Claire stood up and made for the exit. She remembered the time she stole the chocolate and ate it blatantly in front of the security man. Her hand reached into her pocket and she could feel the phone. The temptation was pulling her again. Could she get away with it a second time?

‘Excuse me,’ Claire spoke, pulling the security man’s eyes away from the monitors.

‘Have you got the time? My phone’s batteries have just died.’

She was doing it. She couldn’t believe it. She had the phone in her hand and the security man was giving her the time!

‘Thanks.’

And with that Claire made her way home.

Eleven:

Found Out

Claire returned to school. She felt more at peace, as if some of her emptiness had been filled over the weekend. She visited Solace and finished the chapter she'd started the previous week. It was about a mosquito looking for its next prey. Small in size yet cunning and powerful. Claire felt this way. Her conquest over the weekend had somehow strengthened her. Little did she know her world was about to come crashing down.

At the end of morning registration, she noticed Eric had gone up to speak to Miss Harper. She found this strange. He had never approached the teacher before, and he held her interest. The teacher's eyes then manoeuvred towards Claire, who quickly dropped her own eyes back to her book. *What has he said?* As Eric sat down, he looked directly at Claire and then whispered across the table: 'You're in for it'.

The memory of Eric spilling his water over her beach flashed back into her mind and then she quickly reminded herself of her resolution not to rise to provocations. Claire couldn't concentrate on anything that morning. All she could do was speculate about what Eric had said to Miss Harper. When break time came, he brushed past her before leaving the class saying, 'I saw you take the money'. Claire's face went pale and she wanted to sit back down with the shock of what Eric had just said. She glanced over at Miss, who was busy helping another student finish his work. *I'm going to kill him.* She then left the room intent on finding out exactly what he had told Miss. She felt like she needed to arm herself with something and seeing some scissors left on the table by the door, she grabbed them. She spotted Eric in the far corner of the playground laughing with a group of other boys from the class.

'Eric, can I speak to you?' she called out. She kept the scissors hidden behind her back, wondering why she had even picked them up.

'Go away shrimp,' he retorted. Claire ignored.

'Come here you fool … or are you scared?' she spoke, taunting him.

'Scared of what?' Eric finally replied as he walked over to her, realising she wasn't going to leave him alone.

'What did you tell Miss?' Claire asked.

'That's my business.'

'Did you tell Miss I took the money?'

'Maybe. Maybe not. Did you?'

Claire started to rack her brain, thinking how Eric would have known. Was he calling her bluff? Maybe he saw her that time the boys were playing football. She didn't remember seeing him.

'Well I did,' she finally answered, 'and if you don't tell miss you got it wrong, you'll wish you never lived.' Her hand tightened around the scissors, still behind her back.

'I'm not scared of you,' he challenged.

'… and me of you,' she quickly retaliated, this time showing the scissors held at her side.

'These can cut more than just paper.'

Claire had said enough. Rage was starting to jostle inside her and she wondered if she would ever attack someone in such a way. *What have I become?*

The end of play bell rang, and children started to make their way back to lessons. Claire had just reached the stairs leading back to her classroom when a voice called out: 'Miss May, come here please.' Claire had never been called by her last name before at school and this unsettled her. The head teacher was no more than five feet tall, yet she seemed to tower over Claire, as if she'd grown another two feet.

'Yes Miss.'

'Wait outside my office, I'll be with you in a few minutes.'

Claire waited. She wanted to cry. She had been through every emotion from raw anger to a breakdown in the space of half an hour. Anxiety cast itself over her like a dark cloud. She started biting her nails and then her legs began to jiggle as if drilling for oil. The head teacher eventually came and called her into her office.

'This is not the first time you've been in here this year,' she started. 'I'll give you one chance to own up. If you fail to admit what you've done, we may have to involve the police.' She paused, waiting for the gravity of the situation to sink in. *She must know.*

'We have cameras you know.'

Claire's school life flashed before her: her first day at school; the trips and outings; the performances her mum would religiously come to; the different teachers (some good, some not so good); the friends; and last but not least, Aliya.

There were two weeks left to the end of year six – the end of her primary school. She didn't want to be excluded again. She would miss the school trip and the disco. She would be stuck at home with Dad. This was bad.

'Miss I really don't know why I'm here,' she finally responded. Her body spoke differently. Her eyes were looking down, her body almost curled up into a ball. The head teacher wasn't easily fooled.

'I'm going to ask your dad to come in again. I hope for your sake you are telling the truth.'

Claire wondered what 'truth' she had told. She genuinely wasn't sure why she was in the office and she hadn't said she hadn't stolen the money. She started to wonder if there were cameras overlooking the football area. Did Eric actually tell Miss. What did he actually see?

Dad eventually came into the school. Seeing Claire sitting outside again, he frowned. 'What am I going to do with you?' he said.

He spoke to her without any emotion, as if he was talking to a computer that was refusing to connect to the internet. The head teacher invited him in and moments later Claire was asked to join them. On the table was the plastic bag with the 40 ten-pound notes. She knew it was forty. She had written the number on her calendar next to last Saturday's date.

'Where did this money come from?' her dad asked.

'It's mine', Claire fired back. She wanted to pick it up and walk out of the room. Both her dad's and the head teacher's eyes were burrowing into her. The wall seemed to close in on her too. She felt trapped. There was no easy way out of this one.

'I was going to give it back ... I... I just needed to hold onto it for a while,' she tried to explain.

'You have left me with no choice,' the head teacher began. 'This is a very serious matter. You will be excluded until the end of term. I've asked Miss Harper to have your books and personal effects left at reception. You are never to come back to this school again. Is that understood?'

'Yes Miss. I'm sorry Miss.' With that, Claire's dad got up, apologising profusely for his daughter's behaviour and then marched her out of the office. At the reception, he was handed a black bag which Claire assumed contained her possessions. Yet, the only ones that really mattered were in the art cupboard. As they drove back to the house, Claire's world seemed to rapidly shrink. She felt stripped of everything that had meaning and value. She wondered if Dad had found the phone too. He must have turned her room upside down.

As they got out of the car, her dad told her to go to her room and stay there until he had decided what to do. 'We will need to talk about the phone and my clock,' he said as she climbed the stairs. Claire sat on the edge of her bed looking at the black bag with her school gear. Her thoughts were exhausted. She stayed there, waiting for her dad to call. Outside, it began to get dark.

Twelve:

Prison

'Your summer holidays begin now,' Claire's dad began. He looked like he had rehearsed the message, but his delivery at best was awkward. As he continued to talk about his disappointment in her and how she would have to pay back every penny, he occasionally looked in her direction, but Claire felt that any love he once had for her had long since gone. The lecture went on - his words became monotonous. Claire zoned in and out of what he was saying, keeping her face deadpan. Then, looking out of the window she wondered whether dawn would soon come. She was tired. A couple of times she drifted off, only to be rudely awoken by her dad, who raised his voice spotting her. 'Are you paying attention?' he would say and then continue.

Eventually, her dad's speech came to an end.

'This will be the worst holiday for you. Do you understand? You will not be going out at all. You can't be trusted. You are a disgrace. DO YOU hear me? A DISGRACE,' he finally bellowed out, as if he was spelling the word.

The next day Claire woke up, wondering if the last twenty-four hours had just been a bad dream. It was Tuesday and she needed to be at school. She looked across at her clock and as she registered the time, 10.15am, she realised it was no dream at all. *This can't be happening.*

She opened her bedroom door. The house was quiet. *Dad must be at work.* She ventured downstairs deciding to make a cup of tea to help her wake up. Putting the kettle on, she noticed a note left folded on the kitchen table. It had her name on it:

Claire, I've left this note so that you are clear about your punishment. You are not to leave the house under any circumstances. I can't lock you in, but I have taken your key. If you do leave, I will know. Dad.

It was strange seeing Dad's name placed at the end of the note without a kiss mark or two. She wondered if his love for her had gone forever. She felt more alone than ever.

Claire opened the front door. It was quiet outside. A car rolled past and then she spotted a cat on the neighbour's wall licking itself. *So, if I go, he will know?* She realised that if she decided to leave the house whilst he was at work, she wouldn't be able to get back in, unless she left the front door open and that wasn't going to happen. She then reasoned that she could leave the window at the back of the house slightly ajar, but again that would be a risk. What if they were burgled? Dad would never forgive her. It was all too much. Claire decided to leave the tea and returned straight back to bed. There she lay staring at the ceiling. *What have I done?*

Claire woke up with a start. She could hear drilling noises downstairs. It was now gone seven in the evening. She got up again and this time decided to wash and get dressed. Going downstairs she saw her Dad putting away some of his tools.

'Every window has a lock now, so don't get any ideas,' he announced, as if he'd achieved something great.

She shook her head and didn't bother to respond. Going into the kitchen she remade the tea she was meant to have earlier and poured herself a bowl of cereal. Sitting at the kitchen table she ate slowly, occasionally letting the spoon of cereal pour slowly back into the bowl.

The TV was on in the front room. Dad was watching the news. She had no desire to sit with him and returned to her bedroom.

The next few days dragged by. Claire kept out of her dad's way. It was a simple routine. Get up after he'd left for work. Have breakfast. Watch some daytime TV. Make a sandwich for lunch. Wait for dad to get home. Listen to him pottering downstairs and then the call: 'Dinner's ready'. His half-attempts at making dinner weren't too bad. Claire was grateful for something hot. She would come down and eat it in the kitchen, pop her head in the front room, say 'thanks' and then disappear back upstairs until bedtime. Bedtime was really no time. Claire decided to unplug her clock – after all, she didn't have any appointments to keep. However, she kept her calendar and made a point of checking it each day.

It was painful when she realised she still had the whole of August to get through, but she felt it was important to recognise which day it was – Monday, Thursday or Sunday? People went to church on Sunday. She remembered her dad saying that when he was young, shops never opened. It was quiet. She found this hard to imagine. The only difference she noticed was that at the weekend, there was less traffic in the mornings.

The mornings began to interest her. There were certain sounds she began to identify. The neighbour's cat would rustle against something outside before taking its position on the garden wall to clean itself. Then there was the postman. She could hear him (or her) opening the neighbour's gate and then a few moments later there would be the clatter of letters at her own door. Of course, visits weren't always daily. Sometimes she would hear neither. These sounds were the signal for her to get up – Dad would have left for work by then.

Daytime TV became boring. It was the same heated chat shows, which seemed to be staged and most of it Claire didn't understand – usually stories about people 'sleeping' with each other's best friends and so on. Claire dreaded the thought of getting older and hoped life wouldn't end up being so complicated. Then there were the shows about antiques and places in the sun and then, of course, there was the news.

Claire was missing school: her new friend Aliya, her class – even Eric and all his annoying ways. One morning she woke up before the cat rustled outside. Pulling the curtains back she noticed a couple of children from her school walking past. She recognised them as the twins from year five but didn't know their names. They were walking slowly without talking to each other, all prim and proper. She could imagine their mum fixing their uniform and wishing them a good day, before sending them on their way. Claire's mum always took time to see Claire off. She had started to walk to school towards the end of year four. It was one of the things she missed after her mum was diagnosed with cancer and moved out to live with her sister. Dad never gave her any attention. He was so caught up with himself. Claire was surprised that he was even cooking her dinner in the evenings. Pain started to seep through her body. It was a yearning pain. The pain of loss. Her mind flitted back to the necklace her mum had given her, which was in the box in Solace. If only she had it now. She needed something to bring her comfort. She closed the curtains, as if to stop the pain flooding in. Climbing into bed, she remembered a time when she was sick with fever and her mum stood over her stroking her head with a wet flannel. Claire reached out as if to hold her mum's hand, but there was no one there. No voice of comfort or reassurance. No sweetly smiling face looking down on her. Claire cried.

The days passed, one after the other, seamlessly like the clouds Claire gazed upon beyond the top of the houses on the opposite side of the road. She looked at the calendar and realised it was the last day of school. All her school friends would have been saying their final farewells, signing each other's shirts and autograph books. Hugs and tears would have been shared. She wished she was there. Although she had become distant over the last year, memories of earlier years came back. She smiled. School was fun, at least that was until … Claire didn't want to continue the thoughts. It was just then that the doorbell rang. This was the first time it had rung since she had been excluded. She didn't know what to do. Her dad hadn't given instructions, so she decided to go and open it. She kept the chain on the door in case it was a burglar or some untoward person. That's what mum would have done.

7

Thirteen:

A Visitor

Opening the door and peeping her head through the gap, she stepped back in shock. She looked again and then took the door off the chain.

'Hi. Come in ...' Claire said, her spirit lifting like she'd been in a coma and just come to.

Aliya stepped in.

'Hi Claire,' she said. 'I've missed you.' They hugged. Taking in the moment, Claire stepped back and looked her friend up and down. She was still in her school uniform and Claire reasoned she must have decided to visit her on her way home. She was surprised to see her shirt wasn't signed.

'Wow, this is was unexpected. Do come in,' Claire repeated, not sure what to do next.

'Please take a seat and I'll get you a drink.' Claire was trying to remember how her mum would show hospitality.

'Miss Harper gave me your address. I was told not to stay. She wanted you to have this …' Aliya held up a small bag which Claire took and placed near the door.

Aliya remained standing by the door. Claire's mind was exploding with questions.

'At least stay for a quick drink … I won't keep you longer than I have to,' Claire said, beckoning Aliya in.

Aliya looked behind her down the path to the empty street.

'Okay, but just five minutes.'

Aliya entered the front room, sitting near the door. Claire passed her a glass of lemonade and sat opposite in her dad's chair. Realising her words would have to be few, Claire took a deep breath.

'Aliya, I'm in a real state. My mind is all over the place. I need your help.'

There was an awkward pause. Aliya wasn't sure how to respond. Claire continued.

'I've done some really stupid things. I've stolen money from school. I've shoplifted. I've tricked strangers into giving me money ...'

'I even stole from my dad,' she added, in a whisper. 'I can't handle this prison anymore. I feel like running away, but I wouldn't even know where to go.'

Aliya looked bemused. 'I thought you were ill. No one said where you were. In fact your name wasn't even called out on the register. I asked Miss Harper if I could contact you to see if you were alright. She told me she would let me know. That was yesterday. As I was leaving school, Miss gave me that bag and told me where you live, but I was told not to stay.' Aliya started to shift anxiously in her chair. 'I'll come again,' Aliya said as she got up. 'I must go.'

With that she made for the front door. Claire quickly pursued. 'Thank you so much Aliya. Forgive me. I feel like a real fool.' As Aliya walked down the path, she turned back and looked at Claire with pity. She was like a wounded animal abandoned at the roadside - hopeless and helpless. 'I'll see if I can come again,' Aliya called back and with that she had gone, her sight hidden by the neighbour's tree.

Going back inside, Claire nearly tripped on the bag she had placed by the door. It was a navy blue draw string bag, like the one boys use for their football kit. She picked it up and to her delight, recognised some of its contents.

She pulled out the book *Times Like These* and studied its cover. It hadn't changed: the waters sat calmly cradled by the surrounding mountains. Then there was the torch, the snacks and the alarm clock from the pound shop. She reached further down and found an envelope. It had her name on it. She recognised the writing on the front: 'Miss Claire Lee'. It was from Miss Harper. She opened it and out fell her mum's necklace. She picked it up and examined it. She checked the clasp. Everything looked fine. Her heart started to warm. In fact, the feeling was so intense, she dropped to the floor right where she stood in the hallway. 'Mum,' she cried out. It was a moment's comfort that Claire hadn't experienced for such a long time. A tear trickled down the side of her face. This was a tear of hope. It rolled, straying down her cheek and into the corner of her mouth. She could taste its saltiness. It reminded her of the meals her mum would cook. Always tasty. Always leaving her wanting more.

As she sat there on the floor, she pulled out the letter tucked inside. It was on lined paper that looked like it had been torn out of an exercise book.

Dear Claire, It was a shame you weren't here for graduation. I don't know what drove you to do what you did. I guess we all have our reasons. You have always been a special student. Conscientious, helpful and hardworking.

Claire stopped and reflected. She had forgotten that she had been a good student. She nodded her head, as if to agree, and read on:

I'm hoping this is a phase you're going through – like the book says, 'Times like these'. Bad times and good times pass. They all have their moments but life continues. Use the summer to prepare yourself for secondary school. Do some reading and writing.

Practise your maths. Have fun and keep out of trouble!

p.s. the cleaner found your box in the art cupboard. Interesting! Was it your hideaway? Anyway, she seemed to guess it was a year six pupil's and came straight to me. So, it's our secret. ☺ *Miss Harper*

'Thanks Miss,' Claire whispered. She sat there not wanting to get up. It was all too much after two weeks of nothing. She gathered her stuff putting it back in the bag and placed it in her room, next to the black bag with her 'school stuff', which she still hadn't sorted out.

Lying on her bed, she started to feel real again - like the Claire of old. Her mum's necklace grasped in her hand, she looked out of the window and watched the sun slip out of view.

Good times, bad times, times like these. Tomorrow would be different, she decided. *Tomorrow, the real Claire will be back.*

Fourteen:

Better Days

Claire's alarm clock went off. She knew it was seven o'clock without even looking. She rushed into the bathroom and quickly washed, making it downstairs just in time to see her dad leave.

'Can we have fish and chips tonight?' Claire asked. Her dad seemed surprised to see her up and in good spirits.

'Why sure', he responded, and with that he gathered a few items and left the house.

Claire made breakfast, as usual, and then without stopping at the TV, went back upstairs. She emptied the bin bag and the tie bag so that everything sprawled out over her bed. Some of it was rubbish – a broken sharpener, rubber bands and screwed up bits of paper amongst other things. There were a couple of exercise books, a drawing she'd never finished and a couple of newsletters that she was meant to take home. Eventually the mess had been cleared.

Everything was in its place. *Times Like These* was placed on her bedside table. She found a bookmark – one she had bought from Hasting on a school trip - and placed it next to chapter 10. *Every night I will read this.*

Something spurred Claire on. It was like an invisible hand gently pushing her from behind. She didn't want to sit down and so decided to do some housework. There was plenty to clean. She tried to remember the last time her dad had hoovered. It was some time over Christmas, when his brother's family came to visit. They only stayed for the afternoon, but the way her dad was carrying on it was as if the Royal Family were visiting. Claire thought about a TV show she once watched: 'Keeping up Appearances'. She chuckled to herself, her dad reminding her of the main character: 'Mr May's residence,' she imagined her dad saying as he'd pick up the phone – which he hardly ever did.

Claire dusted, mopped and hoovered, recalling exactly how her mum would do it. It seemed to take forever, but Claire didn't mind. She was occupied.

She felt alive again. It was as if a bit of her mum was living inside of her. She felt connected.

Sure enough, Dad came home. He placed a bag on the kitchen table. Claire knew immediately it was the fish and chips. She had two plates ready and told her dad to put his feet up – she'd even managed to put the TV on so that the news was cued ready for him to watch.

'You seem chirpy today,' Dad spoke. Claire let the words filter through her. It was a nice feeling. She wanted him to continue.

'Let's see what's going on in the world', he said, as the news chimes rang out each headline.

She sat with him as they munched through their takeaway. Claire tried to imagine her mum there too. It was hard as she would insist they watch anything but the news when together.

'Dad,' Claire piped up, 'let's watch something else.' Dad looked at her. 'Yeah, sure … why not,' and with that he threw her the remote control, which slid across her lap knocking a few chips to the floor.

She flicked a few channels and eventually found a drama series. She had no idea what it was, but she felt mum would have approved.

Claire didn't want to lose the moment. As the program finished and some adverts followed, Claire spoke up.

'Dad,' Claire began, looking directly at him. Dad looked up. He had just finished the last bit of fish, caked in batter and was licking his lips.

'Dad,' she said again as if to be sure of his attention. 'I'm sorry for what I did.'

'Don't worry poppet,' he replied. 'We all have bad times,' he added. Claire paused as she thought about her book. *Good times, bad times, times like these.*

'It won't happen again,' she promised.

Their eyes returned to the TV as a new program commenced.

'Tomorrow, we'll go shopping,' her dad offered. Claire smiled. She would do anything to get out of the house. It had been a good day.

The next day, Claire noticed something was different as soon as she stepped out of her room. She could smell bacon. *Dad cooking breakfast!?*

Sure enough, Dad stood there with frying pan and spatula in hand. He looked like he was commanding a ship into port, moving this way and that way placing things onto plates; managing toasters and pots on the stove. It made her chuckle. He didn't notice.

She decided to leave him to it and went into the front room. The TV was already on and the weather report had just started. 'A sunny start with showers later,' *Typical British weather.* Dad called her in and they ate together at the kitchen table. Neither spoke. There was still a wall between them, but Claire was able to see cracks form, with slithers of light pushing through.

The shopping trip was a success. It created opportunities for them to talk – even if it was about things they needed or didn't, as the case may be. Arriving at Aisle 23, Claire spoke:

'Dad, last time I was here I did something really bad.'

He looked up from the crisp section, where he was trying to calculate whether buying a big bag of 24 variety crisps was cheaper than buying four smaller bags of 6.

'I shoplifted.'

Claire picked up a chocolate bar; it was identical to the one she had previously stolen.

'I actually stopped and ate some in front of the security man.'

'You are something,' her Dad responded, a little surprised. He took the bar from her hand and placed it in the trolley, which was almost full.

After they had paid for everything and placed them into bags, they made their way to the exit; Dad suddenly stopped, right by the security and looked at Claire.

'You know what you need to do,' he said abruptly, looking down at one of the bags where he had strategically placed the chocolate bar near the top. Claire looked up at her dad with eyes pleading: 'No'. She wasn't ready. Her heart started thumping and her palms began to sweat.

'Can I help you?' prompted the security man, wondering why the two customers were loitering by the door.

'My daughter has something to confess,' Claire's dad prompted.

'I'm sorry,' she began. 'A few weeks ago, I stole a chocolate bar from your store.' She reached into the bag and pulled out the chocolate bar. She handed it over and apologised again.

'Thank you,' he replied. 'I wish all our shoplifters could be as honest.'

The three of them stood there wondering who would make the next move.

'Now go, before I arrest you for causing an obstruction!' Claire and her dad took the hint and made for the car.

Claire was quiet on the way back. She kept wondering if she really was sorry. Bit by bit she felt all her 'gains' were being lost. First the ten-pound notes, now the chocolate bar. She wondered about the £499 phone. Where was it? What had Dad done with it? Then there was his clock!

That next day, Claire decided to read some more from *Times Like These*:

Chapter 10: Lizard on the Loose

There was something about the room Green Lizard liked. It was a good size. Plenty of places to run around. Plenty of places to hide. It was safe too from the predators lurking in the outside world. Whilst most lizards were green, Green Lizard got his name because he was greener that the others. His greenness glowed so much it was almost fluorescent.

The dressing mirror he lay against shook with such a force that he thought he'd fall off. His suckers clung all the more. His eyes rolled around to see what had caused this tremour. There it was, falling from the sky… he darted sideways, missing its impact. Mr Green scuttled around to the back of the table and lay low.

He stepped out of the shadows and looked down the deserted alleyway. His pursuer wasn't to be seen, but he couldn't relax. He had walked through the same area many times without any trouble. Why was he now being shot at? Who had he wronged? There were noises further down the darkened passage, like dustbins and crates being knocked. He strained his eyes to see, but there was nothing.

The story continued. Mr Green managed to make it back to his flat several streets away. He kept wondering who could be after him. Two shots, one of which he heard whistling past him and striking the wall behind. He locked the door with all three bolts and waited. He didn't know if he could venture out again without becoming an open target. He had to think. He had to be smart. If someone wanted him dead, then he would have to get out of the area – and not by the front door. He opened the bathroom window at the back of the flat to see where it led. It was glazed and just big enough for him to squeeze through. About four feet below, he could see part of a roof, just big enough to stand on. Grabbing a few essentials and placing them in a backpack, which he lowered out first, he made his escape. Mr Green returned to his reptilian form. He found himself outside. Nowhere was safe ... *just keep moving, keep moving!* The story concluded.

Claire placed the book down and wondered if anywhere was safe? And if so, safe from what? This story scared her. She realised that life had many twists and turns, most of which no one could predict. She considered her own situation. It's not that she didn't feel safe. She knew that her dad, despite his many faults, would somehow always be there to protect her. Her house had locks – more now! So why didn't she feel safe. She walked over to the mirror hanging over the TV, imagining Mr Green, the lizard, hanging to the frame: never at peace, not knowing when the next 'blow' would come. It was then that she caught sight of her image. It made her jump. She realised she hadn't taken time to look at herself properly since her exclusion. Her hair was tied back in one, but there was no evenness to it. Her face, while clean, seemed to have formed lines, as if someone had written 'I must not be anxious' over it a hundred times.

Claire didn't want to look anymore, but she forced herself. She remembered a picture she had when she was eight. It was at the seaside and she was in the sea with her mum. They both leant back with their long hair touching the surface of the water. They were both smiling. She wondered where the picture might now be, realising that since her mum's death, she hadn't seen any family pictures around the house at all. The smiles haunted her. They were good times. Happy times. Times together. All that had gone. Looking back at the mirror, Claire wondered if those days would ever return.

Bang!

Claire jumped back in surprise as bits of glass dropped to the floor. She couldn't believe it. Somehow her right hand had lurched forward, with full force and smashed the mirror. She didn't like what she saw she didn't like her image. She didn't like what she had become. It was then that she realised who she wasn't safe from – herself. She had become a monster and the scary thing was that she couldn't predict her next move.

When Dad came home, Claire decided to tell him exactly why the mirror had been smashed. She had cleaned up the mess. All that was left was the frame and the brown papered backing board.

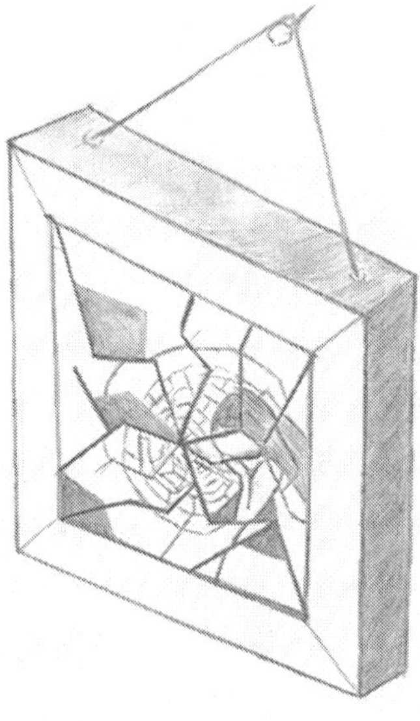

'I don't know what came over me,' she admitted.

'We should try and get you some help,' he offered.

'Maybe,' Claire surrendered. She knew she couldn't go on like this. Back in her room she checked the calendar and counted the days left to starting secondary – 3 weeks and 2 days. *Too long!*

Later that day, Dad informed Claire that he had made an appointment with the doctor for the following morning.

At the GP's, nothing much was concluded, although the doctor suggested that she may be going through a grieving process, after the passing of her mum. He told her to go out more and mix with friends. An appointment was made for them to return in a week's time.

On the way home Dad agreed that keeping her in probably wasn't the best thing for her. He told her that they would have to go out together and suggested the movies. Claire was happy to go out, even if it was with Dad. She didn't have to talk to him! He was probably thinking the same thing.

'Maybe you have a friend who could come and visit?'

'Aliya,' she responded almost immediately. Claire explained that she was new to the country and that she too had lost her mum.

'Problem is ... I don't have her number.'

'Would the school have it?' Dad asked.

'I guess so,' Claire responded, trying not to raise her hopes.

'Leave it with me,' he said, and with that he left the room.

The next day, about an hour after Dad had left for work, the doorbell rang. Claire ran down the stairs, leaping the last three steps as she held onto the banister. *Could it be?* It was. Aliya stood at the door.

'Come in. Come in,' she repeated.

Aliya stepped in. She looked pretty with her jeans and T-shirt and simple hairstyle.

'Hi. I can stay longer this time,' she said.

'I love you Dad.' Claire couldn't believe she had just uttered those few words. Joy was welling up inside - for once he had done something good.

'Come in,' she said again.

They sat in the front room and Claire remained silent, breathing in the moment. Her friend, her good friend, had come back.

Claire spoke, explaining that her dad had taken her to the doctors and it was suggested she was going through a grieving process. Aliya listened with interest. 'In Jamaica,' she explained, 'we don't have doctors for that kind of thing.' Claire asked how Aliya dealt with the death of her mum.

'Well, it took us all by surprise. I'd just come home from my school and my older brother told me to sit down. 'Mum's died,' he said. It took a few days for me to accept it. I carried on going to school and tried to imagine mum at home when I came back. My brother took charge, cooking meals and making arrangements for the funeral. We have a thing called 'Nine Night'. Every night family and friends would gather to eat and drink, and the men would sit and play their dominoes. I found it helped me. At first, I didn't want to talk to anybody, but after about the third night I found I could join in conversations. People gave their condolences, but generally they just chatted about everything and anything. I met family members I never knew I had. When it came to the funeral, I got to see my mum one last time …' Aliya paused. A tear rolled down her face. 'She lay in the coffin. People walked up to it like a pass by, saying a few words or reaching in to touch her hand or shoulder. When it was my turn I could hardly see. I stood on my tiptoes and there she was, looking peaceful but still. There was no life. Her spirit had gone.'

'I guess I've just come to accept it. She's gone and she's not coming back. It's not mine to reason why. She was good to me and I will always love her.'

Claire was impressed with how Aliya talked about her experience. She said it with calm assurance. There was no resentment, no bitterness. She wasn't angry.

'Do you have a picture of your mum?' Aliya asked.

'I think Dad's hidden them all,' Claire answered and then disappeared upstairs without explanation.

Several moments later, she came downstairs smiling. She had a shoe box in her hands.

'It was under my Dad's bed. I remember seeing it when I was looking for some money'. They slipped down onto the floor as Claire started taking out the pictures, carefully explaining each one … where and when it was taken and who was in the picture.

Ten minutes later, Claire looked up:

'How rude of me! I've not even offered you a drink'.

'Lemonade would be great,' Aliya politely responded.

With drinks in hand they continued to look through the pictures. Eventually Claire found the one at the beach, where their hairs had been dipping into the deep blue sea. Looking at it, Claire reached out her finger and touched her mum's face and then let it move over her hair as if stroking it. Tears started to roll down her face. Aliya shuffled around to Claire's side and put her arm around her.

'It's OK,' she whispered. 'You can say goodbye now.'

'I love you mummy. I always will,' Claire spoke. She placed the photo down on the carpet and looked at Aliya: 'Thank you.'

Aliya stood up. 'I'm going to leave you now, but I can come back tomorrow.'

Aliya sensed it would be good for Claire to be alone – for her to say her final goodbyes. She let herself out, leaving Claire to sort through the photos.

Claire spent the rest of the afternoon remembering the good times. She placed all the photos of her mum together at the top before closing the shoe box lid. When her Dad got home, she explained what had happened with Aliya's visit and confessed to taking the box from under his bed. He nodded his head as if to say 'That's ok, I understand'.

Claire decided not to keep any pictures of her mum, respecting her dad's wishes to have them put out of sight. The lid of the coffin had been closed. She had said her goodbyes. Mum was gone. *Just keep moving.*

Fifteen:

Broken

True to her word, the next day Aliya returned.

'Today I have a mission,' Claire informed her. 'I need to admit to a crime and I need your help. I'll explain on the way.' Checking she had the keys Dad had given her earlier that morning, she stepped out and pulled the door firmly to.

As they walked, Claire explained how she wanted to right some wrongs. It was her idea. She had asked her dad about the phone she had stolen and he admitted that he didn't really know what to do about it. He was worried that admitting to stealing it could result in her going to court. Claire asked for it and he gave it back to her. She'd wrapped it in a plastic bag and placed it in her jean's pocket. It felt heavier this time – more than the 6 batteries that had replaced it in its packaging. As they got closer to the store, Aliya stopped and grabbed her arm. Turning to look at her, she asked: 'Are you sure you want to do this?'

‘I have to. What else can I do? I’ll ask to see the manager. My dad told me I could call him, if I needed his assistance.’

Stepping into the store, Claire asked the security guard for the manager and he proceeded to speak into his radio.

‘What’s it about?’ he asked.

‘Stolen goods,’ Claire responded.

Moments later the manager came and invited her to come into an office at the side. Claire asked if Aliya could come too and she agreed. The manager seemed pleasant enough. She was of normal stature, with long blonde hair hanging kindly down both sides of her shoulders.

‘So, what can I do for you ladies?’ she enquired.

‘Well …’ Claire began, ’It’s hard to explain.’ This was going to be hard. Aliya gave her a reassuring look.

‘A few weeks ago, I stole a phone from this store.’

The manager’s facial expression changed. Her hair no longer had its gentle way and her brows narrowed.

'Excuse me one minute,' she said and then left the room.

'What have I done?' Claire said with a look of desperation.

She reached for her phone, wanting to call her dad. The phone refused to connect. There was no reception. She passed the phone to Aliya telling her to get her dad.

The manager walked back in, this time accompanied by the security guard.

'Your friend is going to have to leave I'm afraid.'

Aliya took her cue and left, making the call to Claire's dad as soon as she was back on the street.

Claire remembered the lizard from *Times Like These*. She felt trapped: nowhere to run or hide. She had to face the music.

The manager placed herself down purposefully in her chair. The security man was still standing in the corner of the room.

'So young lady, what is it you've taken?'

Claire pulled the bag out of her pocket, unfolded it and took the phone out, placing it carefully on the table.

'How on earth did you get that!' the manager exclaimed. Claire explained, as the manager jotted down notes in a large book she had opened.

She sat listening, shaking her head as more details were revealed. Any hint of kindness in her had now vanished. The room seemed to get smaller. Claire was struggling to go on. By the time she had finished, her head was so far down she wondered if she could ever hold it up again. The manager whispered something to the guard and he disappeared, only to appear later with the young sales assistant that had attended to Claire.

'Is this the man who served you?' she asked.

Claire looked up. 'Yes Miss.'

She then told the sales assistant to go. Claire felt bad. She wondered if her tricking him had cost him his job. She had taken advantage of his youth and inexperience.

'Well young lady, you have got yourself into a lot of trouble. I've phoned for the police. In the meantime, you may want to think about the consequences of your actions.' She beckoned the security guard and they both left the room.

The room not only became small but dark. Claire thought of the art store cupboard, which she'd named Solace. If only she could escape. If only she could run there. She was trapped. She stood up and started to pace up and down. She could feel anger building inside her. It was the same energy she felt the time she'd smashed the computer screen on the floor and made a dash for it.

Eventually the door opened. Without hesitation, Claire burst forward. She slipped past the manager and then clambered under the guard's legs. She noticed another lady standing nearby. She was uniformed and reached over to grab Claire's arm, but Claire was too quick. Seeing the exit, she ran. She brushed into a couple of customers who were waiting at the till and then suddenly found she could go no further: two arms had wrapped themselves around her. She felt held like a fly caught in a spider's web. The more she struggled, the tighter the hold. She felt confused: it was a familiar hold, one she hadn't experienced for a long time. It was her dad!

'Calm down, calm down,' he kept repeating. The manager, security guard and uniformed woman had now caught up.

Claire burst into tears. Her body went limp. She just wanted to curl up into a ball right there on the street.

'Remember, providence will lead you,' she heard a voice at her side. *Aliya!* She looked up but just saw a blur of colours. She wiped her eyes, but it was still hard to make out anybody. She still wasn't sure what 'providence' was, but she knew it meant she had to be strong. She had to trust things would be OK. Her dad was there. Aliya was there somewhere too.

Claire clambered to her feet trying to fend off the arms holding her. She could hear her dad's voice - it was firm. He was talking to the other adults.

'Come,' she heard him say and then felt his hand holding hers. 'I will look after you,' he reassured her.

They all walked back into the office, but this time her dad sat next to her. He was leaning forward and was asking what had happened when his daughter had come into the store. Claire felt protected. She looked at her dad and started to see him differently. *This is my dad.* She felt warmness towards him. *He may not be perfect, but he's my dad.*

Eventually, the uniformed lady, who turned out to be a police officer, turned to the manager and spoke: 'So what action would you like to take?'

'She should be arrested.'

'Don't you think she's learnt her lesson?' the officer responded.

'The goods have been returned,' she added.

Claire breathed in, taking courage. She stood up and everyone looked her way. The security guard edged towards the door, expecting her to run again.

'I apologised earlier. I am truly sorry. If that's not enough, arrest me.' Claire put her hands forward joined at the wrist, as if ready to be handcuffed.

'I don't think that will be necessary,' the officer replied, looking at the manager once again.

‘Well, considering the item was returned and it’s not damaged,’ the manager eventually murmured, as she examined the phone, ’I guess we’ll leave it at that…but DON’T ever come back into this store. DO YOU UNDERSTAND?’ she shouted, looking at Claire.

‘I understand,’ Claire responded.

Claire gave one last glance at the manager then left. *Maybe I’m not the only one with anger problems.*

Sixteen:

Home

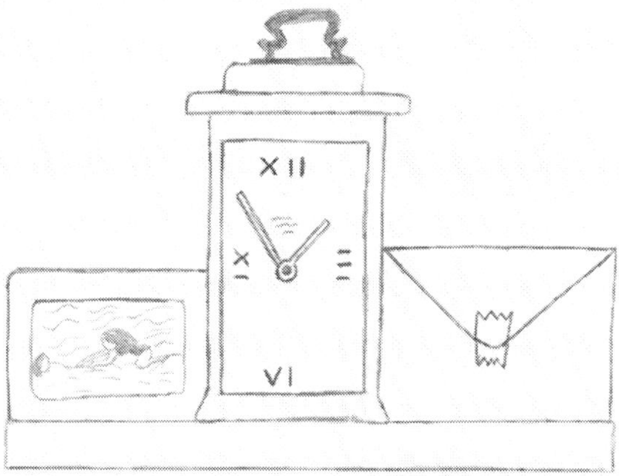

Stepping out of the car Claire felt different. She was home - home, where there was love, security, understanding and peace. Aliya was still with her and asked Claire if she wanted her to stay.

'Yes, but I still have one more thing to do.'

‘Dad, I need to go back into town.’ She looked at her dad, but he didn’t seem too pleased.

‘Don’t worry, I won’t be going near the electrical store!’

‘You need to be back in an hour.’

Claire grabbed Aliya’s hand and made off back down the road. A few roads later, she stopped outside Cash Converters. Looking in, she tried to spot her dad’s clock, but all she could see were phones. Claire chuckled. *I really don’t want to be seeing any more phones today!*

‘Do you know what you’re doing?’ Aliya said, pulling Claire’s arm back and stopping her from entering the shop.

‘Not really,’ Claire responded. Her mind jumped back to Sixth Sense, the observant and sly crow in the *Times Like These* story.

‘Don’t worry, I won’t do anything silly,’ Claire finally spoke and then made her entrance. The door rang a bell. She didn’t remember it doing that last time. They were the only customers there. A large man sat behind the counter and a younger and much slimmer man was to the side, arranging some items in the display. They looked like characters from a comic book.

Claire went up to the counter.

'Excuse me,' she said, 'I need to buy back an item I sold here about four weeks ago.'

The large man stared at her and her friend, waiting for more information.

'It was a gold clock,' Claire continued.

Now standing and without speaking, he pulled a large book out from behind the counter and flicked through the pages.

'We don't get many clocks,' he finally spoke.

'Here it is ... let me see ... ah yes ... a very nice clock too ... gold plated.

He went on to inform her that as it hadn't sold, they would be sending it off to be melted down for its gold content. Claire was relieved that they still had it ... that was until the large man spoke again:

'I'll take £160 for it.'

'Are you crazy?' Claire shot back at him. 'You only gave me £30 for it.'

'£160' he repeated as he closed the book with a bang.

Claire and Aliya left the store downhearted. Claire thought about Sixth Sense again. *He wouldn't walk away like that. He'd find a way.* She was challenged by her thoughts. She didn't want to get into any more trouble, but she believed there was a way. Her mind was now thinking about the other younger man arranging items in the display.

'Aliya, I need your help. We're going to go back into the store, and I want you to distract the man at the counter. Tell him he looks buff or something.'

Aliya gave Claire an incredulous look.

'Just ask him some questions about how much things cost.' Aliya shook her head, but seeing her friend's determination, agreed to give it a go.

They stepped back into the store and Aliya took her position over at the counter. Checking that the large man's attention was sufficiently absorbed, she made her way to the man at the display cabinet.

'You're doing a good job,' she informed him.

'Yep, this is my pride and joy,' he responded. Claire found the response strange, looking at the display, wondering what part he was referring to.

'Yes, nice!' she affirmed.

'Listen,' she went on, 'a few weeks ago there was a clock. Nothing much really.'

'The gold one,' he replied.

'Yes, that's it,' she said.

'I need help,' Claire continued. She then went on to tell him how it was her dad's, a special gift he'd received when he got married. She explained that her mum had passed away and how this was one of the few things they had to remember her by. Claire looked up at Aliya and the large man. Somehow, she was making him laugh. *Good job Aliya!*

The display man looked into Claire's eyes as she continued to explain how she'd sold it to the shop and made an awful mistake.

'Wait there,' he said and then disappeared into the back of the store. Moments later he returned with a bag, which he passed to Claire.

'We've all done silly things before,' he spoke gently. 'Don't worry. I'll sort this. My dad's the manager.'

'Thanks,' Claire said, holding the clock in both hands. 'This means so much to me.'

She called Aliya, who excused herself. Stepping outside, they gave each other high fives.

'Providence provides?' Aliya asked.

'Providence provides!' Claire agreed with a smile and a twinkle in her eye.

On their way back, Claire's dad passed them.

'Fish and chips tonight, love. Are you staying Aliya?'

Aliya accepted. That evening, they sat in the front room. Claire's dad gave her the remote control and she promptly found a Disney movie.

'Have you looked in the cabinet?' Claire asked her Dad.

'Yep … it's complete again,' he responded.

'Have you looked on the bookshelf?' he returned.

There in a silver frame was the photo of Claire with her mum, the one taken at the beach.

'Aliya. Our home is your home. You are welcome at any time,' Claire's dad announced. Claire couldn't believe her eyes. Her dad was being … her dad.

'Dad … you're the best!' The words were hard to speak, but they were true and needed to be said.

'This is home again,' Claire concluded. She hugged her dad and then hugged Aliya.

* * *

Several days later, Claire's dad called her downstairs before leaving for work. He held a white envelope in his hand.

'This,' he said waving the envelope in front of her, 'is for you. Don't spend it all at once.'

Claire opened it eagerly, as if it was Christmas. Inside was a wad of twenty-pound notes.

'School starts in a week's time. You'll need equipment, books and stuff.' It was clear he didn't really know what she needed, but she was grateful.

'I've ordered your uniform. Hopefully it will fit,' he continued.

'Your ban is now officially lifted. You are free to go out as you please.'

Claire hugged her dad and he left for work. On the side table by the door she spotted her keys, still with the Minnie Mouse key ring attached. *That's going to have to go for a start.* She called Aliya and told her to meet her in an hour by the Town Clock – they were going shopping!

In her excitement, Claire couldn't decide what to wear and after trying on the third outfit, decided to stick to jeans and a simple purple top with a flowery design riding on the shoulder. She brushed her hair several times adding gel to straighten it and then threw it into one, brushing it again and flipping it from one shoulder to the other to see which side looked best. She then realised she didn't have any makeup. She looked through her draws but could only find some red nail varnish that had dried up and a stick of lip gloss. *First stop: the make-up store.*

Claire bounded down the stairs, grabbing the keys and envelope. She wished her dad 'bye' and slammed the door. Claire half ran and half skipped as she made her way to town. The air felt different and although the sun wasn't shining, everything was light and full of goodness.

Reaching the Town Clock, she spotted Aliya immediately.

'Let's go to McDonalds,' Claire spoke as she came up behind her, slipping her arm in hers. 'We've got a busy day ahead.'

They sat down with their egg and sausage muffins and Claire held up her bottle of orange juice.

'Here's to good times.'

'Good times and providence,' Aliya responded, and they clunked their plastic bottles together.

Claire counted out the money. There were 11 notes in total, not including the change from their meal. Claire passed 6 of them to Aliya.

'These are for you.'

Aliya passed them straight back.

'I can't,' she said.

'Your choice,' Claire responded, jumping up from the table. Claire had her way. She'd become shrewd over the past few months. Making for the door, she left Aliya, the empty meal wrappings and the 6 twenty-pound notes still sitting on the table.

Aliya gathered them together and placing them firmly in her pocket, followed soon after.

By the end of the day, Claire and Aliya had become more than friends. They were sisters. They didn't need to say it - they felt it. Walking back to the house, they found themselves holding hands, swinging them back and forth. They instinctively stopped as they turned the corner. Looking at each other they smiled and then burst into laughter. Neither knew what was so funny. They were just happy.

Epilogue

Claire lay in her bed, looking up at the ceiling. The thought of starting secondary school had started to worry her. She had her equipment and the uniform, her dad bought her, did fit after all. She had researched every detail of the school from its website. She knew what time it started, what activities and clubs were available, even how to get there: 24 minutes by walking or 11 minutes by bus, with a little help from Google Maps. What she didn't know was who from her primary school was going there too. Aliya was going to an all girls' school in the next borough. Claire's school was mixed. Hopefully Eric wouldn't be there. *Please God, no.*

It was hopeless: she couldn't get to sleep, so she decided to get up and write.

She titled the page: 'Surviving Rage'.

Claire wondered how she would be starting secondary. She thought about the older children, some of who might provoke her. She thought about all the new teachers – one for each subject. Would she get on with them? Then there would be her tutor. What would she or he be like? Would they understand her?

This is my resolve. And she put pen to paper:

1) Solace is a good place to be: a place of safety; and a place for healing. I will find such a place.
2) *Times Like These* has helped me. It introduced me to interesting characters. I will read it and read it again.
3) Aliya was a great friend. No one can ever replace her, but I will find new friends.
4) Eric was a pain, but I've learnt to deal with him. I will be patient and not rise to provocation.

She folded the paper and placed it under her bedside clock. It was now two in the morning. She felt the tiredness gently tugging at her eyes. She put aside her thoughts and reached for *Times like These* for one last read before bed.

Chapter 11: The eagle soars

It was so far down. All she could see was jagged rocks. The wind was still for a few moments before its breeze pushed again against the nest. Her siblings had already departed, and she knew she couldn't stay much longer. Then came the shadow. Her mother's wings spread out as she swooped down. Instinctively she knew what this meant. She clung to the fragile edges of the nest hoping it would hold her.

Her small body and half folded wings morphed away and there she stood before the gates of the city. Macey was a reporter. Her work had been exclusively in Europe and this was the first time she had been in a 'high risk' zone. Armoured cars trundled past.

There was no amount of training that had prepared her for this. One open backed jeep had three soldiers hanging onto the side and she glimpsed a fourth person sprawled out on the deck of the jeep. He was injured, his clothes bloodstained. One soldier held a drip above him.

Security at the gate was ridiculous. Macey was searched by a female guard and her bags were examined at length.

The story unfolded: Macey survived, telling the 'inside' story of life in a war zone. Four weeks later she returned to her comfortable desk in Wall Street, to write up the full story in an editorial series. Her experience had raised her to a new level of reporting and her boss was now looking for her to take an exclusive at another not so glamorous location. This time she was ready.

Morphing back into the little eagle, her mother's nudge as she landed on the nest, was enough to send her tumbling over the edge:

She bounced off a couple of rocks at first and stretched her wings out flapping frantically. This steadied her a little, but then she hit another rock which pushed her further away from the mountain side. It was at that moment that she felt something lift below her left wing. It then caught her right wing too. It was like an invisible hand. She tried to balance herself. Her wings were now fully stretched showing their full plumage. Raising her head, she looked about. She could see the land below, but it wasn't racing towards her as before. Above, she could see the nest and the side of the mountain. She was soaring. With a little movement of each wing she found she could change direction and with a few flaps she rose higher. So this is flying!

Claire put the book down. *I'm ready.* Whatever lay ahead of her wouldn't discourage her. Rage still had many colours, but Claire felt that one by one, she was able to recognise them. Out of her window she saw the sun setting, leaving a trail of colour in the sky. Soon it would all be gone and darkness would reign, at least until dawn broke. Tomorrow is a new day. Each day has its challenges. Claire knew better. She looked one last time at the cover, with the still waters of the lake and ran her fingers over the title: *Times Like These*.

Good Times.

Bad Times.

Times Like These.

And with a little contented smile she snuggled into her pillow and fell into the deepest and sweetest sleep.

Message from the author:

*I hope you enjoyed reading **RAGE**.*

Keep an eye out for the next books in this series:

outRAGE

and

outRAGEous

For more information about workshops, resources

and author bookings visit

www.reading4life.co.uk

Printed in Great Britain
by Amazon

71226425R00090